TRUNDLEBERRY MANOR

1R BOUNCER'S
HOUSE

FIRE
STATION

BLODGER'S
GATEHOUSE

SIGMUND SWAMP'S
HOUSE & BOATHOUSE

FERNYBANK FERRY

XK GRUFFY'S
SHOP

BRAMBLE'S FARM

CHURCH

VICARAGE

RAILWAY STATION

C. HOPPIT'S
HOUSE

POLICE
STATION

N

E

S

COLU

CUB

ARBUCKLE

D0576409

This book belongs to :

Gary Paulson

BROCK THE BALLOONIST

Written & Illustrated by John Patience

Published by Peter Haddock Ltd., Bridlington, England
© Copyright 1980. Fern Hollow Productions Ltd.
Printed in Italy
ISBN 0 7105 0122 6

Brock Gruffy bustled around his little shop,
puffing on his pipe like an old steam engine.
He was trying to tidy the place up, but it
was in such a terrible clutter that it was
an almost impossible task. Brock was
soon distracted from the job when
he came across an enormous cardboard
box which he couldn't remember having
seen before.
"What's this?" he muttered, adjusting his
spectacles to read the label.
"HOT AIR BALLOON"
"How exciting!"

Brock dragged the box (which was very heavy)
out into his garden, and, following the
instructions, soon had the balloon inflated.
It was striped red and yellow and was
absolutely gigantic!

The badger climbed into the basket and untied the
anchor rope, and the balloon floated up into the clear
blue morning sky. Higher and higher it climbed until the
houses of Fern Hollow looked like tiny little models.
Soon Brock began to feel dizzy and decided to bring the
balloon down a little. Unfortunately the silly badger let
out far too much air and found himself speeding towards
the church steeple.
"Oh no!" cried Brock, covering his eyes.

CRUNCH
the basket hit the steeple
and sent it crumbling
to the ground!

Parson Dimly came rushing out of
the vicarage, thinking that there
must have been an earthquake,
and was amazed to see the enormous
balloon floating away across the
River Ferny, with Brock Gruffy
in the basket waving his arms around
and shouting for help.

At last the balloon came down on top of Sigmund
Swamp's roof, crashing into his bedroom and giving the
poor Toad, who was still in bed, the fright of his life.

Soon a crowd of animals had gathered around Sigmund's house, and P.C. Hoppit arrived on his bicycle looking very serious. Of course Brock couldn't afford to pay for all the damage he had done, and P.C. Hoppit had no alternative but to arrest him.

What a terrible thing to happen! Brock Gruffy was locked up in Fern Hollow jail and feeling, as you might imagine, very sorry for himself.

The balloon was now anchored behind the police station where Monty and Spud Tuttleebee peeped out at it from their hiding place in the bushes.

The two mischievous mice had decided that they would like to try flying the balloon themselves.

"Quick," whispered Monty, creeping across to the balloon.

"Jump in and we'll be off before anyone notices."

Once more the balloon
floated up into the sky and,
carried by the wind, quickly left
Fern Hollow far behind.
But Monty and Spud soon learned
that flying a balloon was not as easy
as they had imagined. They were flying
low over an island in the Ferny when the
basket caught in the branches of a crumbling old
tree, and down fell the balloon, taking the tree with it!

"Hey," called Spud, clambering out of the basket. "Look at this Monty."
Beneath the roots of the overturned tree was a treasure chest.
"It must be pirate gold!" cried Monty, lifting the lid and running his fingers through the gold pieces.

When Monty and Spud had recovered from their excitement they realised that they were marooned. The balloon had burst and was quite useless. Luckily Monty knew how to make a fire by rubbing two sticks together, and the unfortunate mice huddled round the flames as it grew dark.

Spud was almost falling asleep, when Monty shook his shoulder and pointed at a light bobbing out in the river. "It's the pirates come back for their treasure!" he whispered.

"No it's not!" cried Spud. 'It's P.C. Hoppit and Sigmund Swamp. Hurray—we're rescued!''

Soon Monty and Spud were
safely back home, and
Mrs. Tuttleebee was tucking
them up in bed.

The next day the treasure was given to Brock Gruffy; after all, it would never have been discovered at all without Brock's balloon. Now the lucky badger had more than enough money to pay for the damage he had done, and so he was set free with a stern warning from P.C. Hoppit not to go messing around in balloons again.

Monty and Spud got a good ticking off from P.C. Hoppit too, but old Brock more than made up for that by making them both guests of honour at a celebration party.

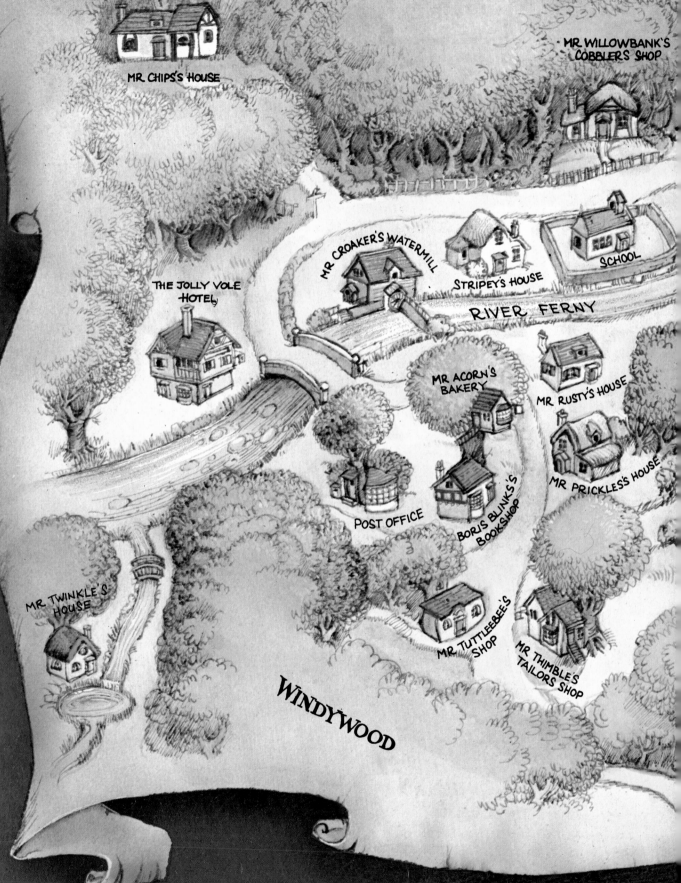

Fern Hollow

MR. CHIPS'S HOUSE

MR. WILLOWBANK'S COBBLERS SHOP

MR. CROAKER'S WATERMILL

STRIPEY'S HOUSE

SCHOOL

THE JOLLY VOLE HOTEL

RIVER FERNY

MR. ACORN'S BAKERY

MR. RUSTY'S HOUSE

POST OFFICE

BORIS BLINKS'S BOOKSHOP

MR. PRICKLES'S HOUSE

MR. TWINKLE'S HOUSE

MR. TUTTLEEBEE'S SHOP

MR. THIMBLE'S TAILORS SHOP

WINDYWOOD